## Dinah the Dog with a Difference

Dinah is different from the other puppies. Her mother is worried. But being different is not so bad. In fact, it makes her just right for a very special job!

Here are some new words that you will read in this book:

**blind** . . . . . . . . . . . . . . . . **not able to see.**
Our neighbor, who is <u>blind,</u> takes the bus to work.

**dog guide** . . . . . . . . . . . **a dog who helps people who are blind.**
The <u>dog guide</u> knew when to cross the street.

**explore** . . . . . . . . . . . . . . **look in new places and for new things.**
Sharon loved to <u>explore</u> the hills.

**Labrador retrievers** . . . . **special dogs that are very smart and have very good eyesight.**
<u>Labrador retrievers</u> have big paws and smooth fur.

**litter** . . . . . . . . . . . . . . . . **a group of puppies or kittens, all born at the same time.**
Paul's dog had a <u>litter</u> of fourteen puppies.

**train** . . . . . . . . . . . . . . . . **teach how to do something.**
Ruth will <u>train</u> her dogs to sit and lie down.

## EASY-TO-READ ANIMAL ADVENTURES:

CATKIN the Curious Kitten          NAT the School Cat
LENNY the Lost Donkey               TOMMY the Timid Foal
HONEY the Hospital Dog              DINAH the Dog with a Difference

---

A Note to Grownups: This delightful "Real Life" animal adventure also introduces young readers to the following themes: being "different" from other children; understanding the value of others as individuals; growing up; and the importance of helping others and of feeling needed.

On page 28, a section called "Things to Talk About" encourages children to explore these themes by talking about them with other children and with adults. The questions in "Things to Talk About" also give adults a chance to participate in the learning - and enjoyment - to be found in this story.

---

Library of Congress Cataloging-in-Publication Data

De Fossard, Esta.
    Dinah, the dog with a difference.

    (Easy-to-read animal adventures)
    Summary: Despite her mother's warning that people
don't want a dog who is different, Dinah finds her
liveliness and curiosity well suited to her new job as a
seeing eye dog.
    [1. Dogs–Fiction. 2. Guide dogs–Fiction. 3. Individuality–
Fiction] I. Bartram, Haworth, ill. II. Title. III. Series.
PZ7.D3394di 1985          (E)          85-14815
ISBN O-918831-45-8
ISBN O-918831-22-9 (lib. bdg.)

North American edition first published in 1985 by

Gareth Stevens, Inc.
7221 West Green Tree Road
Milwaukee, Wisconsin 53223

U.S. edition, this format, copyright © 1985
Text copyright © 1985 Gareth Stevens, Inc.
Photographs copyright © 1973 by Childerset Pty. Ltd.

First published in Australia by Childerset Pty. Ltd. with an original text copyright by Esta de Fossard.

Reading Consultant: Libby Gifford
Series Editor: Mark J. Sachner
Designer: Sharon Burris

Typeset by Colony Pre-Press • Milwaukee, Wisconsin 53208 USA

# Dinah
## the Dog with a Difference

**Story by
Esta de Fossard**

**Photography by
Haworth Bartram**

8-87

Gareth Stevens Publishing
Milwaukee

At first Dinah looked like all the other puppies in the litter. They were all golden Labrador retrievers.

But soon her mother saw that Dinah was different. The other puppies ate good meals.

But Dinah did not like dog food. She liked people food. And she liked to eat alone.

The other puppies stayed home. But Dinah liked to explore.

Dinah found a hole in the wall. The hole was smaller than she was. She almost got stuck.

Dinah played with some stockings. She chewed on them. She even put her head and paws in them. She just loved to learn new things.

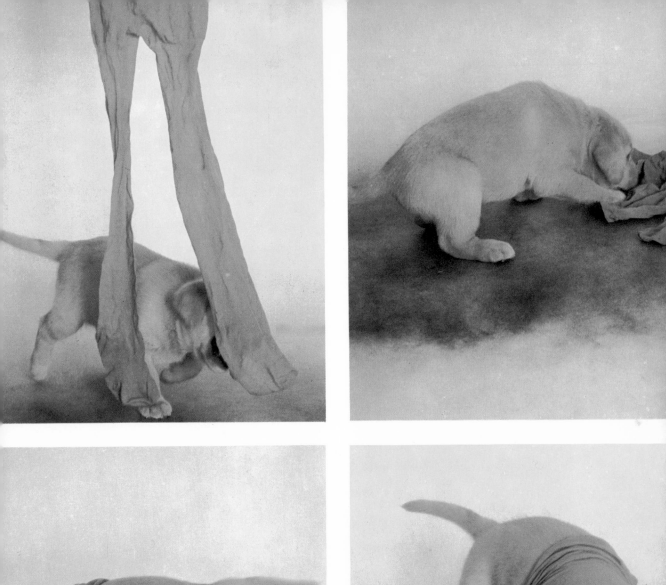

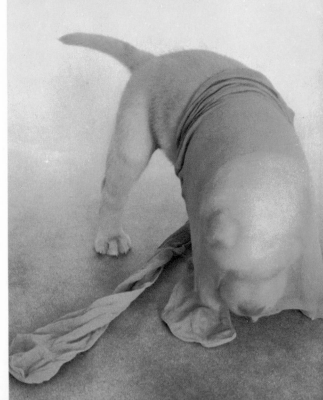

Dinah saw some flowers. She smelled them. Then she tasted them. And then she tipped over the vase and sniffed inside.

Dinah's mother said, "You are different, Dinah. Your exploring gets you into trouble. People don't want dogs who are different."

Dinah's mother seemed to be right.
All the other puppies had new homes.
But nobody wanted Dinah. Dinah was
different.

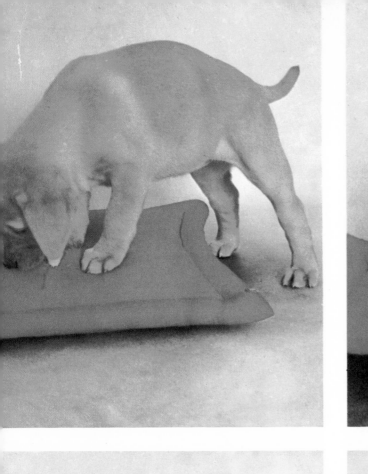

Then one day a man came to see her. "This is just the dog I want," he said. "She is different. She likes to explore. She is not afraid of anything. We need a dog like Dinah. We will train her at our special school. She will be a dog guide."

Now Dinah is a grown-up dog.

She is still different. And she is important.
She is a friend to a man who is blind.
Dinah helps the man go where he
wants to go.

He often pets Dinah. He says to her,
"I'm happy that you are different. That
makes you the best dog for me. You
are the best friend I have."

Dinah is happy, too. She likes helping the
man. And she still loves being different.

## Things to Talk About

Reading can be fun. Talking about the stories we read can be fun, too.

Here are some questions about the story of Dinah, the dog who was different. Now is your chance to talk about how you feel about the story. If you like, show these questions to a grownup you know. He or she will be happy to talk about the questions with you. Now you can have fun reading and talking about Dinah and her adventures!

1. Dinah is a puppy who grows up to be a big dog. How are big dogs different from puppies? How are grown-up people different from children?

2. Look at the pictures across from pages 6 and 8. Dinah likes people food better than dog food. What are your favorite things to eat?

3. What things do you least like to eat?

4. Look at the pictures of Dinah across from pages 16 and 20. Dinah tips over a vase and rips open a pillow. How do you feel when you spill something or break something?

5. Dinah's mother tells her that Dinah is different. How is Dinah different from the other puppies?

6. How are people different from one another?

7. Do you ever feel different from other children? How?

8. Dinah grows up to become a dog guide. And she learns how to help a man who is blind. What does a dog guide do to help a person who is blind?

9. Look at the picture of Dinah and the man who is blind across from page 26. What is the man in the picture doing? How are people who are blind just like people who can see?

10. What things do you help other children with?

11. What things do you often need help with?

12. What things do you help grownups with?

13. How do grownups help each other?

14. Look at the list of New Words on page 1. Can you find these words in the story? Use the Index of New Words on page 30. Can you think of new ways to use these words?

# Index of New Words

**B**

## More Easy-to-Read Animal Adventures that are fun to read and talk about:

### Catkin the Curious Kitten

Sometimes Catkin's curiosity gets her into trouble. But she learns how to be careful. And then her curiosity helps her find out all kinds of things!

### Honey the Hospital Dog

Honey is a very special dog – a hospital dog! With her help, everyone learns how important it is to have good friends.

Honey gets lots of love, too. And she keeps an eye out for trouble!

## Lenny the Lost Donkey

Lenny follows the children to school one day. On the way, he gets lost. He soon finds out how important good friends are.

And he finds out that school is not the only place for learning about things!

## Nat the School Cat

Nat is looking for a home. Some children take him into their school. There he finds the food and love he needs.

Then, one day, the school is dark and the children are gone! What will Nat do?

## Tommy the Timid Foal

Tommy finds it hard to make friends. "What good are friends?" he asks.

Then he meets some animals and a young boy. And he finds out that having friends isn't so bad after all!